Houndsley
and
Catina
and the Quiet Time

Houndsley and Catina and the Quiet Time

James Howe
illustrated by Marie-Louise Gay

CANDLEWICK PRESS
CAMBRIDGE, MASSACHUSETTS

To Mark,
and our quiet times together
J. H.

First edition 2008

Library of Congress Cataloging-in-Publication Data is available.

Library of Congress Catalog Card Number 2007940973

ISBN 978-0-7636-3384-4

2 4 6 8 10 9 7 5 3 1

Printed in China

This book was typeset in Galliard and Tree-Boxelder.
The illustrations were done in watercolor, pencil, and collage.

Candlewick Press
2067 Massachusetts Avenue
Cambridge, Massachusetts 02140

visit us at www.candlewick.com

Contents

Chapter One
Silent White

It was the first snow of the winter.

Houndsley gazed out his window at the silent white falling everywhere. The world had no shadows, only white on white on white.

"It is the quiet time," Houndsley said in his soft-as-a-rose-petal voice.

Catina listened.

"It is too quiet," she said.

"Oh," said Houndsley. "But that is why this is my favorite time of year. In the quiet time, everything stops. I think we may be snowed in."

"Snowed in?" Catina cried, jumping up to join Houndsley at the window. "But this is terrible. What about the concert tonight? I was going to get my whiskers curled and buy a new dress. And we're in charge of refreshments."

"We have all day to bake cookies," Houndsley said. "Your whiskers look fine just the way they are, and you have plenty of dresses you can wear. The stores might not even be open today. It's a storm, Catina. There's nothing to do but enjoy it. Isn't it beautiful?"

“A storm isn’t beautiful,” Catina replied. “A storm means not being able to do all the things we had planned on doing. Oh, no!”

“What is it?” Houndsley asked.

“What if we can’t have our concert? We have been practicing for months!”

“What will be, will be,” Houndsley told his friend. “Let’s enjoy the day. We can still practice, and if there is a concert tonight, we will be ready for it!”

Houndsley returned to his cello.

Catina picked up her clarinet.

Before they began to play, Houndsley said, "Listen, Catina. Can you hear it?"

“Hear what?”

“The quiet. It is almost like music.”

Suddenly, there was a loud crash from the house next door. Houndsley's neighbor Bert was practicing for his part in the concert. Bert played the cymbals.

"Houndsley," said Catina, "I do not think Bert understands about the quiet time."

Chapter Two
The Island

The snow kept falling.

All morning, Catina fretted about her plans for the day.

All morning, Houndsley told her not to fret.

Finally, Houndsley said, “Let’s pretend that we are on an island. We can’t go anywhere. Let’s see, what do we have on the island with us?”

“I don’t suppose we have a whisker curler, do we?” asked Catina.

"No, but we do have books," said Houndsley. He pulled a book from the shelf and sat down on the sofa, patting the cushion next to him. "Let's read poems to each other. I'll start."

At first, Catina had a hard time paying attention. She looked out the window and wished that the snow would stop. But when it was her turn to read, she found a poem that made her laugh.

And then Houndsley read a poem that made her cry.

"I am not a very good writer," she told Houndsley after they had read for a while longer, "but it might be fun to write poems. Even bad ones."

"I think there may be paper and pencils on this island," said Houndsley.

For a long time, the two friends wrote poems and read them to each other.

“I’m sleepy,” said Catina. “My brain is tired.”

“Why don’t you take a nap while I fix lunch?” Houndsley suggested.

“Good idea,” said Catina with a yawn.

* * *

After lunch, Houndsley and Catina baked cookies.

Then they played board games, because there were board games on their island, too.

There were also logs on their island. Houndsley and Catina built a fire and talked about what they saw in the flames. And then they grew still and didn't talk at all.

At last, Catina said, "I think there are dreams on this island."

"What do you mean?" Houndsley asked.

"Oh, I was just dreaming about all the things I would like to do someday. And then I thought that dreaming about them is almost as good as doing them."

Houndsley nodded. "Sometimes dreaming is even better than making plans," he said.

Soon it was late afternoon. The house was growing cold.

"We need more logs," said Houndsley. "I will climb out a window to get some. I can't open my doors because of all the snow."

"I will go with you," Catina said.

Houndsley and Catina almost forgot about getting the logs. They were too busy building snow creatures and making snow angels and catching snowflakes on their tongues.

A sudden *crash* sent them scrambling to get their logs and climb back inside.

As Houndsley rebuilt the fire, Catina returned from the kitchen with a pot of ginger tea.

Another *crash* was heard.

"On the island next door," Catina said, "there are cymbals."

Chapter Three
The Concert

The sound of cymbals crashing was replaced by the sound of a shovel scraping against the sidewalk in front of Houndsley's house.

"Houndsley! Catina!" cried Bert. "It's time to go to the concert!"

Houndsley and Catina looked out to see their friends and neighbors trudging through the snow with their instruments.

"But I have to go to my house and change my clothes," said Catina.

"No one will see a fancy dress under a coat," said Houndsley. "Besides, a concert is for listening, not for looking."

Houndsley handed Catina her coat and a pair of snowshoes.

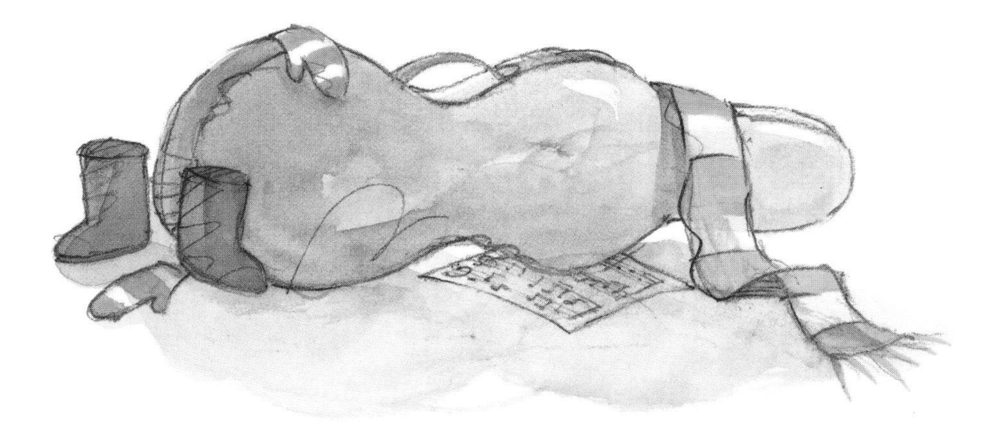

"I have been practicing all day," Bert said excitedly to his friends as they slowly made their way through the snow.

Houndsley and Catina smiled at each other and said nothing.

"I am sad that we have left our island," Catina whispered to Houndsley as they joined the others at the light-strung gazebo in the park. "I like the quiet time."

Houndsley nodded. "I was looking forward to this concert," he said, "but it seems a shame to make noise tonight. Even if the noise is music."

As the musicians took their places in the gazebo, a small audience gathered. The houses around the park had their windows open so that those inside could listen, too.

Without saying a word, the musicians picked up their instruments and began to play so softly that the notes fell on the listening ears like snowflakes on waiting tongues, gently, softly, there for a flicker before melting away.

Houndsley began to worry that Bert would ruin everything. Bert's only part was to play the final note of the final piece of music. *How awful*, Houndsley thought, *to end the evening with a crash.*

But when the last note came, it was not a crash or a clash or a boom or a bang. It was the closest that cymbals can come to silence. It sounded like a chime in the wind. It lingered and floated and fell into the quiet time.

For a long while, no one spoke. No one moved. Everyone just sat and listened to the silence. Some may have dreamed.

When they finally started making their way home, Catina asked, "May I stay at your house tonight, Houndsley?"

"May I stay, too?" asked Bert.

"Of course," said Houndsley. Thinking about the refreshments they had forgotten to take to the concert, he added, "We may have to eat a lot of cookies."

Catina and Bert didn't mind. Eating cookies would be a perfect way to share the quiet time together.